# THE BUSINESS OF BEING A MUSIC INFLUENCER

BY KAITLIN SCIRRI

CAPSTONE PRESS
a capstone imprint

Capstone Captivate is published by Capstone Press, an imprint of Capstone.
1710 Roe Crest Drive
North Mankato, Minnesota 56003
www.capstonepub.com



**Library of Congress Cataloging-in-Publication Data**
Names: Scirri, Kaitlin, author.
Title: The business of being a music influencer / Kaitlin Scirri.
Description: North Mankato, Minnesota : Capstone Press, 2021. | Series: Influencers and economics | Includes bibliographical references and index. | Audience: Ages 8-11 | Audience: Grades 4-6 | Summary: "Are you always looking for the newest bands and singers? Do you love to talk about music and share your musical opinions with others? Then you might have what it takes to be a music influencer. Learn about social media marketing and basic economics, and discover what it takes to become a music influencer, all while staying safe and having fun"— Provided by publisher.
Identifiers: LCCN 2020034874 (print) | LCCN 2020034875 (ebook) | ISBN 9781496695390 (hardcover) | ISBN 9781977154989 (pdf) | ISBN 9781977156600 (kindle edition)
Subjects: LCSH: Music—Marketing—Juvenile literature. | Social media —Vocational guidance—Juvenile literature.
Classification: LCC ML3795 .S23837 2021 (print) | LCC ML3795 (ebook) | DDC 658.85—dc23
LC record available at https://lccn.loc.gov/2020034874
LC ebook record available at https://lccn.loc.gov/2020034875

**Image Credits**
Getty Images: Carol Yepes, 26, Jeff Spicer, top right 11, JKevin Mazur/Fox, bottom right 11; iStockphoto: GoodLifeStudio, 38, ljubaphoto, 18, RicardoImagen, 39, veerasakpiyawatanakul, 44; Newscom: Mairo Cinquetti/ZUMA Press, middle left 11, SNAP/ZUMAPRESS, 17; Shutterstock: Amnaj Khetsamtip, 16, Anterovium, Cover (squares), Cesare Andrea Ferrari, 40, East pop, 31, George Rudy, 9, iego Cervo, 7, insta_photos, 4, Kemedo, 43, LightField Studios, 14, Marish, Cover (music), Motortion Films, 21, PrinceOfLove, 15, Rashad Ashur, Cover (icons), Rawpixel.com, 13, 28, 41, Sonias drawings, Cover (icons), Sutipond Somnam, 23, TheVisualsYouNeed, 24, weedezign, 36, YAKOBCHUK VIACHESLAV, 32, Yuricazac, 34

**Editorial Credits**
Editor: Peter Mavrikis; Designer: Brann Garvey; Media Researcher: Morgan Walters; Production Specialist: Tori Abraham

All internet sites appearing in back matter were available and accurate when this book was sent to press.

Printed and bound in China. 5047

# CONTENTS



Words in **bold** are in the glossary.

# GET PAID TO HAVE FUN!

The camera is rolling. The beat is thumping. One of your original songs plays in the background. The latest album cover art from the hottest new artist is flashing on the screen. Everyone is tuning in to hear your thoughts about the music, the cover art, and the artist. Everyone wants to know if you like it, recommend it, or have any fun inside information to share. They also want to hear your music and find out where to buy it!

You are hanging out at home, wearing a T-shirt with your logo on it. You are smiling for the camera, ready to talk about the latest music. Best of all—you are getting paid for it! You are a music influencer.

CHAPTER 1

# WHAT IS A MUSIC INFLUENCER?

Traditionally, you had to work in the music industry to make money from music. But today you can earn **income** by becoming a music influencer.

A music influencer uses **social media** to share videos and **posts** about music. Some influencers talk about other artists' music. Some make their own music. And some do both. Music influencers don't have to be adults. Even kids can get in on the action!

## Fast Fact!

The influencer industry made around $2 billion in 2017 and around $8 billion in 2019. It's estimated to earn around $10 billion in 2020 and $15 billion by 2022!

Influencers create content to share with others. That includes videos, photos, blog posts, and more.

## Earning Income

Music influencers earn money in a number of ways. One is through advertisements. Ads may be short videos that play before the influencer's YouTube video starts. They may also be small videos on the side of their website. Influencers set up the ads and get paid by companies when people view and click them. Companies may also want influencers to promote an artist or album. They pay influencers to create a post about it. This is called a paid post.

## Costs and Benefits

Thinking of getting into the biz? Being a kid influencer—also called a *kidfluencer*—has **costs** and **benefits**.

Creating videos and posts takes a lot of time. One cost is having less time to do other things, such as hanging out with friends or playing sports. Earning money is a key benefit. You would have money to spend and could save for your future. Some kidfluencers have earned enough to pay for college before they even start high school! Other benefits could include enjoying free products from brands and access to the latest music.

### Fast Fact!

In 2019, 82% of U.S. teens said they listened to music every day. On average, they listened for a total of more than two hours.

## Long-term Opportunities

There is plenty of room to grow as an influencer. With cell phones and tablets, people can watch videos and view posts while on the go. You can reach people anywhere, at any time.

More people today stream videos online than watch TV. This means there's a whole world out there looking for something to watch. You can offer entertainment while growing your business and earning money.

In 2019, 81% of Americans owned a smartphone. That's a potentially big audience for influencers!

## Why Influencing?

So why do people tune in to influencers? Parents like learning what's popular with kids. Kids enjoy seeing the interesting posts influencers make and hearing their opinions. Good influencers can also feel like trusted friends.

People like being influencers because they make money talking about their favorite things! They get to be creative. They get to reach people. Sometimes they become famous too. Some music influencers even get their own record deals!

### Top Influencers

Influencers can focus on different areas. They may choose fashion, toys, gaming, music, and more. Top social media platforms used by music influencers are TikTok, YouTube, and Instagram. Top kid music influencers include Sophia Grace, Jacob Sartorius, and MattyBRaps.

**Sophia Grace**, 16 years old, began influencing online at age 8

- More than 3 million TikTok followers
- More than 3 million YouTube subscribers
- More than 1 million Instagram followers
- More than 230,000 Twitter followers

**Jacob Sartorius**, 17 years old, began influencing online at age 12

- More than 22 million TikTok followers
- More than 3 million YouTube subscribers
- More than 9 million Instagram followers
- More than 1 million Twitter followers

**MattyBRaps**, 17 years old, began influencing online at age 7

- More than 3 million TikTok followers
- More than 13 million YouTube subscribers
- More than 3 million Instagram followers
- More than 840,000 Twitter followers

CHAPTER 2

# GETTING STARTED

So you've decided to become a music influencer. Before you start posting, you'll need to make some decisions and set up your business.

First, choose an audience. Who do you want to influence? Other kids or adults? Maybe both? This is called finding your target audience. Learn about your target audience. Do they interact more with video posts or photo posts? What kind of content do they like?

You should also decide if you want to focus on one type of music or several. Once you decide, find reliable resources about the latest artists and releases. These resources could be websites dedicated to music news or musicians.

## The Competition

Your **competition** is other music kidfluencers. Spend some time watching their videos and looking at their posts. Learn what you do and don't like about their content. Then you can think about how to be different. Having a hook that makes your posts unique will help you stand out.

### Fast Fact!

MattyBRaps decided to focus on rap music as an influencer. Rap was his hook—and it worked! Today, he has more than 13 million YouTube subscribers.

Dream of being a producer or musician? How can influencing help you reach that goal? What steps can you take now?

## Business Goals

Setting goals is important for your business. Think about what kind of posts you want to create. Do you want to review others' music for money? Do you want to interview musicians? Maybe you want to create music of your own. Having goals clearly outlined will keep your business on track.

Lawyers and accountants help you follow laws and do what's best for your business. This can help avoid problems later on.

## Building Your Team

To get your business going, you might want the help of different people. A lawyer can look over any legal documents. An accountant can help with bank accounts, expenses, and taxes. Once you gain a following, you might want the help of an agent. An agent works with you to find new opportunities to grow the business.

Making content is a lot of work. It involves writing, filming, photography, and editing. Will you be a solo creator, or will you want a team to help?

## Age Limits

If you're younger than 18, you cannot start a business by yourself. You'll need an adult, such as a parent or guardian. The adult will be able to sign legal documents for you. They will also be able to help with banking. Your parent can open a business bank account for you. Using a business bank account makes it easier to track things that are bought for the business. This includes buying new music or paying for music streaming services.

Coogan Accounts are named after Jackie Coogan, a popular child actor in the 1920s whose parents spent almost all his earnings.

### Coogan Accounts

Some states require a special bank account for child performers called a Coogan Account. Fifteen percent of the child's income must go into this account. The money stays there until the child becomes an adult. But these accounts are not required for kidfluencers. This is because they work at home with their parents. There are currently no laws to protect the money made by kidfluencers.

You'll also need a parent's help creating online accounts. Many social media platforms, such as YouTube, require users be at least 13 years old. TikTok users need to be at least 16. If you're under the age requirement, your parent can help you create an account. But then your parent needs to be in charge of it. This means your parent will monitor your activity and upload content.

## Naming the Business

Not all influencers use their real names online. Some create a catchy business name. Set up social media accounts as soon as you land on a name. If the exact name is already taken, that's OK! Use a similar one for your user name, but try to keep it the same across all social media platforms.

You should also consider buying a website address with the name in case you decide to set up a business website. A website can act as a central link to everything you have online.

### Fast Fact!

The first viral video was quickly shared around the internet in 2009. It showed a little boy acting silly after visiting the dentist. Today the video has received more than 139 million views.

## Investing

To get your business off the ground, you'll need to **invest** in it. There are different kinds of investments. One is money. New businesses need money to get started. You and your parents can invest your own personal money. You might also consider **investors**. Investors are adults who give you money for your business. Investors hope your business will become successful. When your business starts making money, investors earn part of the income.

Some new businesses take a loan from a bank. If a bank loans you money, you have to pay it back over a set amount of time. This could be months or years. You also have to pay **interest**. Interest is money that is paid on the loan amount. If you take out a loan, you will end up paying back the bank extra money because of interest.

Another important investment to think about is time. Decide how much time you want to spend on your business. Do you want to create new content every day? Do you want to work just on the weekends? Will you need to stop doing other activities in order to have time for influencing?

## Taxes

All businesses must pay taxes, and that includes kidfluencers. Taxes are money paid to the government. The amount of money owed is based on the amount of money earned. You need to carefully track all money earned and spent on the business. Ask an adult to help record your costs and income. An accountant could also help with this.

## Business Expenses

Business expenses are things that are bought for the business. An expense could be equipment, such as a camera for making videos. It could also be paying for music subscriptions. Sometimes you might have to pay a fee to use certain music in your videos. It's all part of running your business! Business expenses can usually be subtracted from taxes. So it's important to track all business expenses correctly.

Keep track of receipts! Subtracting business expenses, such as equipment, from taxes will save your business money.

# Online Safety

Sometimes people try to bully influencers online. These bullies may leave mean comments on your videos. Others might try to contact you privately. You should never give out personal information such as your phone number or location. Make sure to talk about online safety with your parents or guardians. They can help you plan how to handle these situations.

Many social media sites have ways of reporting and blocking bullies. But if you ever feel unsafe, tell a trusted adult.

You should also be careful of how you act online. As an influencer, you have the power to become a bully too. So be respectful online. Don't make unkind remarks on others' posts. Acting like a bully could damage your **reputation**. Music companies may not want to work with you. You want to be known for your great content, not for being a bully.

## The Children's Online Privacy Protection Act (COPPA)

Many kids watch influencers on social media. A law was passed in 1998 to protect children online. The law stops websites from collecting information about kids. This means websites can't collect or share kids' names, addresses, or information about the videos they watch. Influencers must follow the rules of the COPPA law. These include labeling any videos created for kid viewers.

CHAPTER 3

# MAKING MONEY

Influencers have many options for making money. But before you start getting paid, you need to have great content that people want to tune into.

So what should your content focus on? Music influencers may talk about musicians, songs, and concerts. But you don't have to stop there. You can talk about any topic related to music. You can even share your own music if you have some.

Be sure you have all the equipment needed for making videos and other posts. Have a space to work too. Will you film videos at home? Will you use your bedroom or another area, such as a basement or a garage? Having a space to create will help keep things organized.

It's a good idea to have more than one video ready to post. This way, posts can be scheduled in advance. So if you get sick and can't film one day, the video can still go live. Regular posting lets followers know they can depend on you for new content.

## Equipment Needed

- Camera for videos and photos
- Camera stabilizer
- Cell phone
- Computer
- Editing software
- Internet connection
- Lighting kit
- Microphone
- Tripod

Performing someone else's music, not just playing a recording, still may require permission from the copyright holder.

## Copyright

All influencers need to follow rules and laws for their posts. A challenge for music influencers is **copyright** law. A copyright protects music. It stops someone from using a song without permission.

### Fast Fact!

Listening to music activates the brain's pleasure center and releases a chemical called dopamine. The same chemical gets released when eating tasty food!

You don't have to play music during your videos. You can talk about songs, albums, and artists instead. But if you want music in your videos, you must get copyright permission before you can use someone else's music. This is difficult to do. Ask a lawyer for help with copyright permissions.

Social media platforms look for copyrighted songs. Videos found using them are usually deleted. Another option is using music from the platform's own music library. YouTube offers a library of songs and sound effects that can be used in videos.

## TikTok and Copyright Law

TikTok is a social media app for short videos that often have music. Copyright law also applies to TikTok videos, but TikTok has agreements with music companies. These agreements allow certain songs to be used in TikTok videos. TikTok users who use other copyrighted music may have their videos deleted. TikTok is also a place for new artists. Many artists ask TikTok to make their songs available for videos. These artists hope their music will become popular. They hope to get music deals and earn money from their music.

# Ads and Paid Posts

Once you've begun posting and gaining followers, it's time to start making money. One common way is with ads. A popular ad service is Google AdSense. You can use it to place ads on your website or YouTube channel. When someone watches or clicks one of the ads, you make money!

## Making Money on YouTube

**Ways to Earn:**

- Ad income
- Channel membership—followers pay to access special content
- Merchandise shelf—showcases products available for sale on video pages
- Super Chat and Super Stickers—special features for sale during livestream chats
- YouTube Premium subscriber income

**Requirements:**

- Be at least 18 or have a parent or guardian help you
- Follow YouTube's content rules to ensure your posts are appropriate
- Have more than 10,000 subscribers for merchandise shelf
- Have more than 30,000 subscribers for channel memberships

Signing up for AdSense is free, but if you're younger than 18, an adult must create and manage the account.

Paid posts can also help you earn money. This is when a company pays you to post about their products or services. It may be a video post or a series of photos. For example, you may be contacted by a concert arena. They might want you to promote a show. Music companies or artists may also pay for posts. They might want you to promote a new album. Sometimes companies pay influencers to host giveaways for items such as concert tickets.

Influencers must also let followers know when they've received something to try for free, even though they've not been paid.

There are special laws for paid posts that all influencers must follow. One law says you must clearly label paid posts. This means using labels such as "paid advertisement" where viewers will see it right away. Additional labels such as **hashtags** may be added at the beginning of the post. These could be #sponsored, #ad, #paidpost, or #advertisement.

There is a difference between paid posts and honest reviews. Clearly labeling each post is helpful for followers. It helps them understand when you were paid to talk about an album or when you honestly like and want to promote it.

## Brand Partners

Influencers can also earn money by becoming a brand partner. Brands might be clothing or retail stores. You can partner with them to help sell their products. You can do this by placing links on your website and social media pages. You can also post brand links in your videos. When a viewer clicks on the link, they are sent to the brand's website. If the viewer makes a purchase, you may earn money from the sale.

### Fast Fact!

MTV aired its first music video on August 1, 1981. It was the first TV channel dedicated to music 24 hours a day and helped shape people's musical tastes.

## Decision Making

Influencers have to make many important business decisions. You have to weigh the pros and cons of each one. For example, there are pros for having paid posts. Earning money is a big pro. You might also receive free music and gain followers.

There are also cons to paid posts. A con could be negative responses from viewers. They might not like an artist or an album you're promoting. As a result, some viewers might stop following your account. Another con could be the risk of losing followers who only like honest reviews. Some followers don't like to see paid posts.

# Early Music Influencers

Before there were social media influencers, disc jockeys (DJs) influenced what songs were played on the radio. If a DJ loved a song, it was played often and made money. If they didn't like a song, it didn't get played. The following DJs helped pioneer music influencing on the radio.

## Herbert Rogers Kent

- DJ from 1944–2016
- The Guinness World Record holder for longest running on-air DJ

## Alan Freed

- DJ during the 1950s
- Helped popularize the term "rock and roll"

## Casey Kasem

- DJ from 1970–2004
- Inventor of the *American Top 40* radio show

## Howard Stern

- DJ since 1982
- Controversial DJ who popularized "shock jock" radio

## Promoting the Business

Followers help you earn money through views, shares, and clicks. You shouldn't focus on posting to just one of your social media accounts. Share posts across all of them! For example, don't limit a YouTube video to just YouTube. Post it to Twitter or Instagram too. Or share a clip on TikTok.

Being active on multiple social media sites allows more chances for people to see and interact with your content.

Some viewers prefer certain social media sites over others. Using several sites will help grow your audience. A larger audience means the chance to make more money.

To reach new people, you can also use paid promotions. This means paying to have posts appear in feeds. Your posts will show up for your followers, but they'll also show up for other people. The promotions appear as photos or videos when users scroll through their feeds. They are usually on the home page and have "sponsored" or a similar label.

Paid promotions can help point people to your channel. It might help grow your audience, but it costs money. A paid promotion is an investment. It should be considered carefully.

## Fast Fact!

Around the world, there are 3.8 billion active social media users. Young people have an average of 9.4 social media accounts each.

## Paid Subscriptions

Paid subscriptions are another way to earn money. Followers sometimes become really loyal to an influencer. They aren't just followers. They are fans! They are sometimes willing to pay a regular fee for extra content. This may include early looks at upcoming videos. It could also be special content such as behind-the-scenes footage or extended videos.

### Streaming Services

There are many music streaming services. These include Spotify and Apple Music. Some people pay monthly fees for the service. Others purchase songs and albums. Both types of payments allow the user to listen to music for fun. They do not give permission to use the music in online videos and posts. If you purchased a song or album, you still need copyright permission to use it in a video.

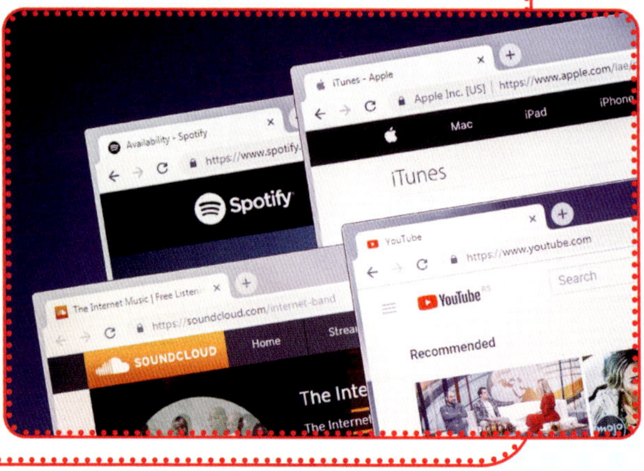

## Working Together

As a new influencer, you should try reaching out to established influencers with large followings. Ask if they will work with you. Together, you can make crossover videos. This is when two influencers help promote each other's channels. For example, MattyBRaps has teamed up with music influencers Chloe Channell and Alex Blue. This helped him reach new viewers. It also helped promote Alex's and Chloe's channels to MattyBRap's audience.

CHAPTER 4

# GROWING YOUR BUSINESS

You're sharing unique and fun music opinions. You've built an audience. You're making money. Where do you go next? It's time to amp up your business.

The stage is set for success! Get ready to rock your music influencing career.

## Stakeholders

Some people have a special interest in your business and helping it grow. They are called stakeholders. They may be investors who put money into your business. They could be adults who help with day-to-day activities. Stakeholders may ask for updates. They may want to know about your business income and stats.

Many social media platforms offer tools to track stats. Stats—short for *statistics*—are things such as the number of views, likes, and clicks on a post. For example, YouTube offers channel stats. These identify a channel's top videos and the total number of users who viewed and interacted with the channel over a set number of days. You can also track the number of followers and watch hours. Tools like this can help you provide updates to stakeholders. They can also let you know in which areas you are doing well and where you can improve.

Keep in mind you aren't just the business owner. You are also a stakeholder. As your business grows, remember to take care of yourself too. This means getting enough rest and keeping up with schoolwork. It also means spending time with friends and family. You should balance your work life and personal life.

## Sales and Marketing

One way to grow your business is by selling products. These could be things such as T-shirts, bags, stickers, and more. Be sure to put your business name or logo on them. This is a form of **marketing**. Marketing means letting others know about your business.

When fans wear a T-shirt with your name on it, other people may ask them about it. They may look you up and become a fan too. Selling products can help you earn extra income and help you gain more followers. This also helps you grow and earn more!

## New Content

Another way to grow your business is by adding new types of content. Say you've mostly reviewed albums. You might think about doing something different. You might attend live music events. Maybe you'll review album artwork. You might even start creating and sharing your own music. Adding new content may draw new watchers and followers.

### Fast Fact!

YouTube is one of the most popular influencer platforms. More than 1 billion hours of videos are watched every day.

## Looking Ahead

Once you've had success as a music influencer, where will you go next? Will you make a long-term career out of the world of influencing? Maybe you'll explore other interests and focus on fashion, toys, or games. You may decide to invest in other influencer businesses. Or maybe you'll study marketing or advertising in school. Your influencer business can lead to many different opportunities.

Ready to get started?

# Timeline

1988 1992 1996 2000 2004 2008 2012 2016 2020

**1995** – 18 million American households have internet access, though only a small number actually go online.

**2000** – Americans regularly use the internet to purchase products and communicate through email.

**2005** – The first YouTube video is uploaded.

**2005** – Music streaming service Pandora launches online.

**2006** – Twitter launches.

**2008** – Music streaming service Spotify launches online.

**2010** – Instagram launches.

**2013** – More than half of all Americans own a smartphone.

**2014** – The app Musical.ly launches, allowing users to lip-sync to music videos.

**2018** – Musical.ly merges with the app TikTok.

**2020** – YouTube has more than 2 billion users worldwide.

# GLOSSARY

**benefit** (BEH-nuh-fit)—something you gain, such as money or fame

**competition** (kom-puh-TISH-uhn)—others in the same business you are in

**copyright** (KOP-ee-rahyt)—the right by law to copy, sell, and publish a product or work

**cost** (KOST)—something you give in exchange for something else, such as time or money

**hashtag** (HASH-tag)—a tag to group online posts and aid in searches; starts with #

**income** (IN-kuhm)—money someone earns or is given on a regular basis

**interest** (IN-ter-ist)—a charge a borrower pays a lender

**invest** (in-VEST)—to give something such as time or money to a business, person, or cause

**investor** (in-VES-tor)—someone who gives time or money to a business

**marketing** (MAHR-keh-ting)—the activities and things that are part of telling others about a business, product, or event

**post** (POHST)—something shared to social media, such as photos or a video

**reputation** (rep-yuh-TAY-shun)—what others think about you

**social media** (SOH-shuhl MEE-dee-uh)—websites people use to share content

# READ MORE


Andal, Walter. *Finance 101 for Kids: Money Lessons Children Cannot Afford to Miss*. Minneapolis: Mill City Press, 2016.

Juilly, Brett. *Make Your Own Amazing YouTube Videos: Learn How to Film, Edit, and Upload Quality Videos to YouTube.* New York: Racehorse for Young Readers, 2017.

National Geographic Kids. *Turn It Up! A Pitch-Perfect History of Music that Rocked the World*. New York: National Geographic Children's Books, 2019.


# INTERNET SITES

*Ducksters Education Site: Money and Finance*
ducksters.com/money/economics.php

*The Mint*
themint.org/kids/

*NetSmartzKids*
netsmartzkids.org/

# INDEX